13

GHOSTLY TALES

Edited by FREYA LITTLEDALE

Illustrated by WAYNE BLICKENSTAFF

AN
APPLE
PAPERBACK

SCHOLASTIC INC.
New York Toronto London Auckland Sydney

For reprint and adaptation permission, grateful acknowledgement is made to:

Dell Publishing for "The Thing at the Foot of the Bed," "The Dare," "Wait Till Martin Comes," and "The Golden Arm" from *The Thing at the Foot of the Bed, and Other Scary Tales*, by Maria Leach. Copyright © 1959, 1981 by Maria Leach.

Doubleday & Co., Inc., for "The Ghost Dog of South Mountain" by Frances Carpenter from *Wonder Tales of Dogs and Cats* by Frances Carpenter. Copyright © 1955 by Frances Carpenter.

Aileen Fisher for "The Witch in the Wintry Wood" and "Ghost in the Orchard" by Aileen Fisher from *Spooks and Spirits and Shadowy Shapes*. Published in 1949 by E. P. Dutton. Copyright and used by permission of the author, who holds all rights.

Holt, Rinehart and Winston, Inc., for "The Wild Ride in the Tilt Cart" from *Ghosts Go Haunting* by Sorche Nic Leadhas. Copyright © 1965 by Leclaire G. Alger; for "The Ghosts from the Graveyard" (originally titled and published as "The Bogles from the Howff") from *Heather and Broom* by Sorche Nic Leadhas. Copyright © 1960 by Leclaire G. Alger.

Houghton Mifflin Company for "The Most Haunted House" adapted from Chapter 7 of *Spooks of the Valley* by Louis C. Jones, copyright © 1948 by Louis C. Jones.

McIntosh and Otis, Inc., for "The Trunk in the Attic" by Adele De Leeuw (originally titled "A Strange Surprise") from *Spooks and Spirits and Shadowy Shapes*. Copyright 1949 by E. P. Dutton & Co., Inc.

Story Parade, Inc., for "The Railroad Ghost" by Murray T. Pringle, copyright 1954 by Story Parade, Inc.

The Texas Folklore Society for "The Ghost with One Sock" based on "The Half-Clad Ghost." Copyright 1932 by The Texas Folklore Society.

ISBN 0-590-43933-2

12 11 10 9 8 7 6 5 4 3 2   0 1 2 3 4 5/9

Contents

Wait Till Martin Comes

by Maria Leach

THAT big house down the road was haunted. Nobody could live in it.

The door was never locked. But nobody ever went in. Nobody would even spend a night in it. Several people had tried, but came running out pretty fast.

One night a man was going along that road on his way to the next village. He noticed that the sky was blackening. No moon. No stars. Big storm coming for sure.

He had a long way to go. He knew he couldn't get home before it poured.

So he decided to take shelter in that empty house by the road.

1

He had heard it was haunted. But shucks! Who believed in ghosts? No such thing.

So he went in. He built himself a nice fire on the big hearth, pulled up a chair, and sat down to read a book.

He could hear the rain beating on the windows. Lightning flashed. The thunder cracked around the old building.

But he sat there reading.

Next time he looked up, there was a little gray cat sitting on the hearth.

That was all right, he thought. Cozy.

He went on reading. The rain went on raining.

Pretty soon he heard the door creak, and a big black cat came sauntering in.

The first cat looked up.

"What we goin' to do with him?"

"Wait till Martin comes," said the other.

The man went right on reading.

Pretty soon he heard the door creak, and another great big black cat, as big as a dog, came in.

"What we goin' to do with him?" said the first cat.

"Wait till Martin comes."

The man was awful scared by this time, but he kept looking in the book, pretending to be reading.

Pretty soon he heard the door creak, and a great big black cat, as big as a calf, came in.

He stared at the man. "Shall we do it now?" he said.

2

"Wait till Martin comes," said the others.

The man just leaped out of the chair, and out the window, and down the road.

"Tell Martin I couldn't wait!" he said.

The Trunk in the Attic

by Adele DeLeeuw

Doug's parents were waiting for him when he got off the train after his summer at camp.

"You've grown," his mother marveled.

"You're as brown as a nut," his father said.

Doug picked up his bag and followed them to the car.

"We have a surprise for you, Doug," his mother told him.

"A dog?" he asked eagerly.

"Maybe that too, in time," his father replied. "If we get the house we're after, you can have a dog. And room for a shack and a tent in the yard."

"Boy!" Doug cried. "Are we going to *move?*"

They told him about it as they drove through the town's quiet streets. Old Mr. Waltham wanted to sell his house.

4

"That funny-looking place on Spruce Street?" Doug asked with real disappointment.

"It needs paint," his mother admitted, "and a lot of repairs."

Doug thought it would be great to have a house after living in a crowded apartment all his life. But the Waltham house! Doug didn't think much of that spooky-looking place.

He thought even less of it now, as their car pulled up in front of the old house. In the deep shade of the drooping trees, the place looked gloomy and neglected. The paint was peeling and the porch steps sagged.

"Mr. Thomas, the real-estate agent, is coming later," his mother said. "But Mr. Waltham said it would be all right for us to look the place over by ourselves before Mr. Thomas gets here."

They went up the walk and across the creaking porch and pressed the bell. They could hear it pealing through the house. After a long time, the door opened a crack and an old man peered out at them.

"We're the Hornes, Mr. Waltham. We've come to see your house."

The old man hesitated. "Well, come in then," he said, opening the door grudgingly. "I'm busy, but . . ."

"We'll be as quick as we can," Mrs. Horne promised. "I think it's going to storm, and we do want to get home before it breaks."

Inside the house it was so gloomy they could scarcely see. Doug stumbled over a torn place in the carpet, and a cloud of dust flew up. The rooms looked as if they hadn't been dusted for a long time. Paper hung in patches on the walls. There was a musty smell in the dark, shadowed corners.

Doug strained, trying to see in the gloom.

"Could we have some lights, sir?" Doug's father asked.

"No lights. Foolish to have lights in the daytime."

Mr. Waltham hurried them from room to room, limping ahead and muttering to himself. In the dining room Doug saw a strange mound under the table-cloth. Something on the table had been covered up. What was it? There were thick books piled on chairs, and a dish of red liquid stood on the window sill.

Doug wished they would get out of the house. He didn't like it. But his father had stopped in the den, in front of the fireplace. The wall above was almost covered with weapons — knives with thin, shining blades, curved scimitars with jeweled handles, and deadly-looking daggers. There was even a cutlass.

"What a wonderful collection of weapons, sir!" Doug's father cried.

"Yes, it's a good one," said the old man. "Took me years to get it together. I like knives . . . they have their points!" He gave a sudden dry cackle. "And every one of 'em has a story. See that dagger up there?"

"The one with rust on it?" Doug asked.

"Rust? Not rust, young man." Mr. Waltham's voice grew suddenly loud. "That's blood, boy. Human blood."

"Wh-whose?" Doug asked with a dry throat.

The old man shrugged his shoulders. "I've . . . forgotten," he mumbled. "Come along, come along. I can't be all day at this."

Doug stared at his thin back and bent shoulders. Human blood! Doug was sure the old man knew all about it. Why wouldn't he tell?

They went upstairs and along the narrow hallway, from one bedroom to another. They were dark rooms — full of old-fashioned furniture, and faded curtains and carpets. Doug tried to remember all that he had ever heard about Mr. Waltham. It wasn't much. The old man had lived by himself for years. Not a hermit, exactly, but seldom going out and seldom having anyone in. "Eccentric," people said. That meant that a person was odd, queer, different from other people. But Mr. Waltham was supposed to be harmless. Just an old man who liked to live by himself. And now, he said, he wanted to get rid of the house because it was too hard to take care of.

Maybe, Doug thought, that was just a story. Maybe that wasn't the real reason at all.

Doug grew tired of following his parents about while they measured the rooms and checked on windows, walls, and fireplaces.

He wandered back into the narrow hall, pausing before a door that was slightly ajar. He pulled the door open and saw a steep stairway that led to the third floor. He started to climb the stairs.

"Boy, where are you going?" the old man said suddenly. He was right behind Doug.

"Just — up here," Doug said, turning quickly.

"You don't want to go up there. It's only an attic — full of dust and junk," Mr. Watham told him.

"An attic!" Doug's eyes brightened. "I like attics."

"May he go up, Mr. Waltham?" his mother asked. "I think he's bored, hearing all these details. You won't disturb anything, will you, dear?"

But Doug was already bounding up the steps, two at a time.

It really *was* an attic. And almost completely dark, except for two small dormer windows, partly open. The unpainted floor creaked at every step, and low, dark rafters slanted to the peaked roof. But it was full of things — broken-down tables and chairs, an old lamp, and a couple of statues. There was a sofa with sagging springs, and piles of big black books. And there were boxes and trunks that looked very old. Doug wondered what was in them.

It was growing darker outside. Through the little windows the sky looked stormy, and a wind was rising. Doug felt a mounting sense of excitement. What *was* in those boxes and trunks? He wasn't supposed to disturb anything, but it wouldn't hurt if he just

8

took a look. It was getting darker all the time, and soon he wouldn't be able to see anything.

He lifted the cover of the box nearest him. For a minute he just stared, not believing his eyes. *The box was full of bones!* Long bones, short bones, thick and thin bones. They didn't look like ordinary animal bones. Maybe they were the bones of a person! Why would Mr. Waltham hide a box of *human bones* in his attic?

Doug shivered and hurriedly closed the box again. He shouldn't have looked. But perhaps it was a good thing he *had* looked. There was something mysterious and queer about this house, and about Mr. Waltham too. What else lay hidden away in this attic? Doug remembered how the old man hadn't wanted him to come up here in the first place. Was there something even worse in one of the trunks that Mr. Waltham was afraid Doug would find?

Doug's knees felt wobbly, and he wanted to run downstairs. But a feeling stronger than fear kept him in the attic. If there was something wrong here, he had to warn his parents. Doug looked around and noticed that a piece of cloth was hanging out of one of the big trunks. The rusty hinges screeched as he lifted the lid. Inside there seemed to be only a crumpled white rag that had been carelessly stuffed in the trunk. But then Doug saw it was loosely wrapped around something.

Gingerly he pulled at the cloth, and then he stared,

unbelieving. For there, stretched out on the bottom of the trunk, was a skeleton — *a human skeleton!* The empty eye sockets glared up at him from a fleshless skull full of grinning teeth.

So this was what Mr. Waltham hadn't wanted him to see!

Doug felt his hair rising. Sweat gathered on his forehead; at first he couldn't move. Then, tearing his eyes away from the gruesome skeleton, he ran toward the attic door. The wind was howling in the trees outside, and a gust of air rushed past him. Just as Doug reached the door, it slammed shut in his face.

Thunder growled close by, and rain spattered against the half-opened windows. In a flash of lightning, Doug groped for the door handle and turned it. *The door would not open.*

He stood there, breathing fast. The wind had blown the door shut, and the lock had sprung on the other side. And there was no key. *He was locked in the attic with the skeleton!*

He had to get out. He had to warn his parents. He had to get them away from this terrible old man who killed people and put them in trunks until their flesh was gone and only their bones remained.

Doug pounded on the door. Would they hear him above the noice of the thunder?

Then he heard his mother scream. Her voice rose high and frightened in a shriek of pain and fear.

11

What had happened to her? Where was his father? What was old Mr. Waltham doing?

He had to get out, *he had to!*

He ran to the dormer windows. Rain beat on him as he leaned out. There was a narrow ledge, and beyond it a drainpipe ran down to the ground, past a second-story window. Doug hoisted himself out on the ledge, winding his arms and legs tightly around the lead pipe.

If only he weren't too late! He shinnied down the drainpipe; the pelting rain soaked his shirt and plastered his hair over his eyes.

At the second-story window, Doug stopped and looked in. His mother was leaning against the mantelpiece, holding her head. His father was bending over her. He couldn't see Mr. Waltham, but another man was standing in the room. It was Mr. Thomas, the real-estate agent.

"Let me in!" yelled Doug. "Hey! Let me in!"

He pounded on the window, and Mr. Thomas looked up and saw him.

They ran to the window then, opened it, and pulled him in.

"What in the world — his father began.

"I heard Mother scream," Doug cried. "What happened?"

"I hit my head on the wall bracket, dear, just as the lightning flashed," his mother said. "You know how silly I am about storms, anyhow."

"Oh — gosh!" he said. "I thought — I thought —"

His mother was safe: that was the main thing. But he still had to warn his parents. "Look," he said hoarsely. "We've got to get out of here."

"As soon as the storm lets up, we'll go," his father promised.

"No, right now. And you've got to tell the police. He . . . that man" — he pointed to Mr. Waltham — "kills people and puts them in trunks!"

"Douglas!" cried his mother, shocked. "You're hysterical. You don't know what you're saying."

"Yes, I do," he said stoutly. "I opened a box and it was full of bones — human bones. And in a trunk I found a skeleton — a whole skeleton — of somebody he must have killed. Maybe *that's* why that knife downstairs has blood on it. And that's why he didn't want me to go up in the attic. Maybe he's got others . . ."

"That's enough, Douglas!" his father said sharply.

Surprisingly, Mr. Waltham was chuckling, and so was Mr. Thomas.

"What an imagination the boy has!" Mr. Waltham said. "Reminds me of my son."

"I don't blame you for getting excited, young man," said Mr. Thomas, "even though I think you've been watching TV too much. But you see, Mr. Waltham's son is a doctor. In fact, Mr. Waltham is going out to Arizona to live with him. Those bones and that skeleton were among the doctor's prize posssessions when he was a medical student."

"And I never could bear to throw anything out," Mr. Waltham added. "That's why the house looks this way."

Suddenly Doug felt a little silly. He sat down on the bed. "Well, gosh," he muttered, "why doesn't anybody *tell* me things?"

His father clapped him on the shoulder. "Think of the thrill you would have missed," he said.

The Railroad Ghost

by Murray T. Pringle

*I*T WAS a spooky night. As the crack British express train raced through the chilly darkness, fog began to close in around it. It was just the sort of night anything could happen — a night one might even expect to meet a ghost.

Now running a train isn't easy any time, but on this particular evening it was really hard work. Fog pressed in on the speeding train from all sides, like thick folds of velvet. Even with the powerful headlight stabbing the darkness ahead, the engineer had to strain his eyes to see the track.

He was very much annoyed at the fog, because today of all days he wanted to make a record run. And the reason was that Queen Victoria herself was among the several hundred passengers on the train.

Suddenly a horrified gasp escaped his lips. Dead ahead, and outlined in the brilliant beam of the engine's headlamp, a figure in a black cloak stood in the middle of the tracks waving its arms frantically! The engineer made a desperate grab for the brakes and brought the express to a screeching halt.

After quieting the excited and frightened passengers, the trainmen got out to investigate. They searched and called, but there was no sign of the mysterious figure who had flagged their train.

Who had he been, and why had he stopped the train? The crewmen were puzzled. They decided someone had been playing a joke. Even the engineer was almost convinced that it had either been somebody's poor idea of a joke or his imagination playing tricks. But he wasn't absolutely sure.

Just to make certain, he swung down from his cab and walked up the tracks. Suddenly his face grew pale and his heart beat wildly. There, a scant two hundred yards ahead of the stopped train, he found a washed-out bridge! The whole thing had toppled into a swollen stream. If it had not been for the mysterious flagman, the train would have plunged into the stream, killing passengers and crew.

While the bridge and tracks were being repaired, the train crew made another search, but they could not find the slightest trace of the strange figure who had saved the train.

Not until the train reached London safely was the mystery solved.

Lying at the base of the locomotive headlamp, the engineer found a huge dead moth. Most people would have brushed the insect off and thought no more about it. But the engineer held the insect in his hand and frowned thoughtfully.

Then he did a strange thing. He wet the wings of the moth and carefully pasted it to the glass of the headlamp. Then he climbed back into the cab of his engine and switched on the light.

"Ah!" he cried triumphantly. "I thought so!" For as the bright beam stabbed ahead into the darkness, there appeared once again the "phantom" the engineer had seen earlier. But now the "arms" weren't waving wildly. They were still.

The mysterious rescuer had been this huge moth! Somehow, in the few seconds before the train reached the wrecked bridge, it had flown into the beam of the headlight. And because in the dense fog the trapped insect had resembled a cloaked figure waving its arms, many people — including the Queen of England herself — had been saved!

Did this really happen? Well, if you're ever in London, go to the Museum of Natural History and ask to see the "Victoria Moth." You will be shown a huge moth in a glass case — the moth the British call the Phantom Flagman!

The Dare

by Maria Leach

*O*NCE there was a bunch of youngsters sitting in front of a fire telling ghost stories and trying to scare each other. There had been a funeral in the village that day. An old man had been buried that afternoon — an old man noted for his crankiness and cussing. The boys used to torment him, just to hear him rage in helpless fury.

One of the group said if anyone walked on the old man's grave at midnight, he would reach up and grab him.

"Oh, don't be silly! No such thing!" said a boy named Jim.

"Well, I dare you!" said another.

"I dare you!"

"I dare you!"

They all joined in.

"All right!" said the bragging one. I don't believe in ghosts. I'll do it."

"I dare you!"

"I'll do it, and I'll stick my jackknife in the grave! And you can all come see it after midnight, if you dare."

So the party broke up.

Just before midnight, the boy named Jim started for the graveyard. It was awful quiet. The tombstones made long shadows in the moonlight. He was pretty scared. But he could not back out now, so he went on.

Could the old geezer reach up and grab him, he wondered? He wished he had not been so smart and taken on this dare.

But he went on.

He came to the grave. He took out his jackknife and opened it. He knelt down and jabbed it blindly into the mound over the grave.

Then he started to get up and run home. But he could not move! *Something* had grabbed him. *He could not budge from the grave.*

An hour after midnight, the boys went fearfully to the graveyard to see if Jim had left his jackknife sticking in the grave.

When they got there they saw Jim, by the light

of the moon, lying in a little heap on the new-made mound.

In his haste and panic he had thrust the knife through his own coattails. He had pinned himself to the old man's grave and had fainted from fright!

The Wild Ride
in the Tilt Cart

by Sorche Nic Leodhas

THERE was a lad named Tommy Hayes, and a more likable lad you'd never hope to see. Tommy was the sort to take his fishing very seriously, so when a Scottish friend invited him to come up to his place in the Highlands for a visit, and be sure to bring his fishing gear, Tommy was delighted. He'd always heard the fishing up where his friend lived was extra fine, but he'd never had a chance to try it before. So right away he sent a telegram to his friend to say he was coming and what time they could expect him to get there. Then he packed up his fishing gear and a few clothes in his bag, and off he went.

He stepped off the train just about nightfall into the midst of a teeming rain, with the water coming down in bucketsful and sloshing all over the place.

The very first thing he discovered was that nobody had come to meet him. The station was on the edge of a small village, and there wasn't a soul in sight except for the stationmaster, and he was inside the station keeping out of the rain.

Tommy couldn't understand it; he'd sent the telegram in plenty of time. He went in and asked the stationmaster if he had seen anyone in the village from his friend's place, thinking maybe they'd had an errand to do and would be coming along for him later. But the stationmaster said that nobody at all had come over from that way for as good as a week. Tommy was surprised and maybe a little bit annoyed, but he settled down in a corner of the station to wait for somebody to come and fetch him. He waited and waited and waited, but nobody came at all — and after a while he found out why. The stationmaster came out of his bit of an office with a telegram in his hand. "This is for the folks up where you're going," he told Tommy. "Maybe you'd not mind taking it along, since you're going there yourself."

Tommy didn't have to read the telegram to know that it was the one he had sent to his friend. Well, that explained why nobody had come to meet his train. And what was more, nobody was going to come. Since the telegram hadn't been delivered, they wouldn't know at all that he was there.

"Och, well, 'tis a pity," said the stationmaster.

" 'Twas early this morn I got it, and I'd have sent it along, had anyone been passing by that was going in that direction. But what with the weather and all, there's few been out this day, and what there was, was bound the other way."

Well, being a good-natured lad, Tommy couldn't see any sense in making a fuss about it. He'd just have to find a way for himself to get where he wanted to go.

The stationmaster was sorry for Tommy, but he could give him no help. There was nobody in the village who'd be able to take Tommy to his friend's house that night. Two or three of the folks had farm carts, but the beasts were all put up for the night and folks were all in their beds. They wouldn't be likely to take it kindly if Tommy woke them out of their sleep.

"'You could stay in the station overnight," the man said. "You'd be welcome to do so, if you liked to. Happen there'll be someone along on the morrow going the way you want to go."

"And maybe not," said Tommy, not feeling very hopeful. "No, if I'm going to get there at all, I can see I'll have to walk."

"Aye," the stationmaster agreed. " 'Tis a matter of five miles."

"That's not too bad," said Tommy, determined to be cheerful.

"Mostly up- and downhill," said the stationmaster

glumly. "The road is rough. And 'tis raining hard."

"It can't be helped," said Tommy. "I'll just have to make the best of it." He picked up his bag and started out into the rain. The stationmaster came to the door and pointed out the road Tommy was to take. Tommy had gone a little way when the man called out after him. "Have a care for old Rabbie MacLaren! No doubt he'll be out on the road this night."

That didn't mean a thing to Tommy, so he just plodded along through the rain.

The stationmaster had told him no lies about the road. Tommy couldn't remember having trod a worse one. It was up- and downhill all right. Tommy toiled along, splashing through the puddles and slipping on loose pebbles with the rain pouring from the back of his hat-brim down inside the collar of his coat. He was beginning to wonder if the fishing was going to be fine enough to pay for all the trouble he was going through when he heard the sound of cart wheels rolling up the hill behind him.

He stopped and turned to look, and although it was growing dark he could make out the vague shape of a tilt cart coming toward him. It had a canvas top stretched over some sort of framework; and Tommy thought to himself that if he could get a lift, he'd be out of the rain at any rate. He set his bag down and stood in the middle of the road, waving his arms and shouting.

"Will you give me a lift up the road?" called Tommy.

The driver did not answer, but the cart came on swiftly, bumping along over the ruts in a heedless way. As it came up to him, Tommy called out again. "Will you give me a lift?"

The man in the cart didn't say "Aye," but he didn't say "Nay." The cart kept on rolling along, and Tommy had to pick up his bag and jump to the side of the road to keep from being run down.

"I'll pay you well," cried Tommy as he jumped. He felt rather desperate. The tilt cart was his only hope, for he doubted if he'd have another chance to get a lift that night. "I'll pay you well!" said Tommy again.

The driver did not answer, but it seemed to Tommy that the horse and cart slowed down a little. Tommy took it as a sign his offer had been accepted. He picked up his bag and ran after the cart, and hopped in beside the driver without waiting for the cart to come to a full stop.

As soon as Tommy was in the cart, the horse picked up speed again. The creature didn't seem to be minding the roughness of the road in the least. It brought the cart up to the crest of the hill at a good round pace, and when they started down the other side, the horse stretched its legs and fairly flew. The cart bounced and bumped and jolted over the ruts, and Tommy's teeth chattered with the shaking

27

he was getting. All he could do was hold fast to the side of the cart and hope for the best. The cart wheels threw out sparks as they hit the stones that strewed the road, and every now and then a big one sent the cart a foot or more in the air. Uphill and downhill went Tommy with the cart, hanging on for dear life and expecting to land any minute in a heap in the ditch with horse, cart, and driver piled on top of him.

He plucked up enough courage after a while to attempt to implore the driver to slow down. He turned to look at the man beside him. What he saw took the words out of his mouth. It wasn't so much the sight of him, although that was bad enough. He was the hairiest creature Tommy had seen in his life. A wild thatch of hair grew over his head and down over his ears, and was met by a long grizzled beard that almost covered his face and blew in the wind as if it had a life of its own. But that wasn't what struck Tommy dumb. With all that hair in the way Tommy could not be sure of it, yet he'd have sworn the man was grinning at him. Tommy didn't like it. He felt that grin was full of a peculiar sort of evil, and it gave Tommy such a queer feeling that he hurriedly turned away without saying a word.

Just at that moment the road made a turn, and he saw at the side of it, a little distance ahead, a great stone gateway. Tommy knew from the stationmaster's description that it was the entrance to his friend's place.

He gave a great sigh of relief. "Pull up!" he cried to the driver. "This is where I get out."

But the driver made no sign of stopping, and the horse went racing past the gate. Tommy rose in his seat, shouting, "Stop!" Just then the cart wheels hit some obstruction in the road, and Tommy, taken unawares, lost his balance. Over the side of the cart he flew, and landed in the road on his hands and knees. By the time he pulled himself together and got to his feet, the cart was out of sight, although he could still hear the horse's hooves pounding down the other side of the hill.

Tommy would have liked to have had a chance to tell the fellow exactly what he thought of him, but it was too late for that. The cart was gone, and Tommy's bag had gone with it, but at least he hadn't paid the driver. Taking what comfort he could from that, Tommy limped back to the gateway and up the drive to his friend's house.

Tommy's friend was terribly surprised when he opened the door at Tommy's knock, and saw him standing there on the doorstone. But when he saw the plight Tommy was in he asked no questions. He hurried Tommy up to his room and saw that he had a good hot bath and found him some dry clothes to put on.

When Tommy came downstairs again, warm and dry and feeling a hundred times better, he was so relieved to have arrived safely that he was prepared to treat his whole experience as a joke. He handed over the telegram and told his friend he didn't think much of the telegraph service in the Highlands.

Tommy's friend had several other guests staying with him, and they all gathered around Tommy now to hear the story of his mishap.

"Och, Tommy lad," said his friend. " 'Tis a long road and a bad night for walking."

"Did you walk all the way?" asked one of the guests.

"Well, no," said Tommy. "But I wish that I had. I got a lift from one of your wild Highlanders. I never had such a ride in my life before, and I hope that I never shall again. And to top it all, the fellow went off with my bag."

"I wonder who it would be?" asked Tommy's friend. "Not many would be traveling in weather the likes of this at night. The road is bad enough at best. A bit of rain makes it terrible."

"I'll grant you that," said Tommy. "The fellow was driving a tilt cart."

"A tilt cart!" exclaimed another man. "Och, they're none so common hereabouts. The only one I call to mind is the one belonging to old Rabbie Mac-Laren."

31

"Now that you mention it, I remember," said Tommy. "That was the name of the man the stationmaster told me to have a care for. I suppose he meant that I was to keep out of his way. How I wish I had!"

There was a dead silence for all of five minutes. Then Tommy's friend asked, "What sort of man was he to look at, Tommy?"

"An old man, I'd say," Tommy told him. "He had more hair on his head and face than I've ever seen on a human being before. It probably looked like more than there really was of it, because it was so tangled and matted. Of course it was too dark for me to see much of him."

"What was the horse like, Tommy?" asked his friend.

"Not what you'd call a big beast," Tommy answered. "In fact, he was somewhat on the small side. But how he could go! That horse would make a fortune on a race track. We bumped and thumped along at such a pace that I expected both wheels to fly off at any minute."

"'Twas old Rabbie MacLaren, to be sure!" said the guest who had asked about the tilt cart. "He was always one to be driving as if the devil himself was after him. There's a bad spot a mile further on, over the hill. If you miss the road on the turn there, over the cliff you go to the glen below. Old Rabbie came tearing along one stormy night and missed the turn and went over."

"Went over!" Tommy exclaimed. "It's a wonder he wasn't killed!"

"Killed?" repeated the other man. "Of course he was killed. Old Rabbie's been dead for a dozen years."

It took Tommy a minute or two to get through his head what he was being told. Then all of a sudden he understood.

"Dead!" screeched Tommy. *"Then I've been riding with a ghost!"* and he fainted dead away.

The next morning one of the villagers brought Tommy's bag up to the house to see if it belonged to anyone there. He'd found it lying in the glen at the foot of the cliff, below the road. It was the good stout sort of bag that is strapped as well as locked, so all the harm that had come to it was a scratch here and there.

Tommy had recovered from his fright by that time, so they took him out and showed him the place where old Rabbie went over. They told Tommy he was lucky that he left the cart where he did, for when it got to the bad spot the tragedy was always re-enacted, and over the cliff again went the old man with his cart and his horse. There had been some folks who got a ride with old Rabbie, expecting to reach the village over beyond the next hill, who had found themselves below the road in the glen instead. A number of them had been badly hurt, and two or three had never lived to tell the tale.

Tommy suffered no ill effects from his experience. To tell the truth, he was rather proud of it. And as he took his fishing seriously, he didn't let the ride with old Rabbie spoil his holiday. He stayed on to the end and fished all the streams in the neighborhood, and had a wonderful time.

But for a long while after he went home to London he couldn't sleep well on stormy nights. As soon as he turned out the light and closed his eyes, he started to dream that he was riding wildly over that rough, stony road in the tilt cart with the ghost of old Rabbie MacLaren.

The Ghost with One Sock

retold by Freya Littledale

*O*NCE there was a man who died with only one sock on. After the funeral, he kept coming back to his old house. Every night he came back at the stroke of midnight. His wife was so scared she moved from that place. But he found her. So his wife moved again.

She kept on moving, and he kept on coming back. One day she couldn't stand moving any more. So that night she asked him, "What is it you want? Why do you keep haunting me?"

"Please," he said, "could I have my other sock?"

So she gave him the other sock, and to this day he has never been seen again.

The Most Haunted House

by Louis C. Jones

U P in the Hudson Valley, in New York State, the folks like to gather round the fire on a winter's night and swap stories about the country thereabouts. There's one that Seth Carter tells. Seth runs a garage on the road that goes over to Washington County. He says the story is true, and he can even show you the place where it happened. This is how he tells it:

A few years ago, a young fellow and his wife decided to go into the antique business. They had an old station wagon, and they'd drive up into the mountains and buy up all the old chairs and cribs and tables and dishes and glassware they could pile into the car. Then they'd bring all the stuff to their shop here in town, and fix it up and sell it to the summer people. Sometimes they'd be back in the mountains two or three days before they'd get a load. They made a kind of vacation out of it.

This time I'm telling you about they'd been back up in Washington County, north of here, and they'd been three days going over the little mountain roads. They had a good pile of stuff — butter-churns, beds, a saddle-maker's bench, and I don't know what all. It got dusk, and they were close to lost when their headlights began to flicker. The road was very steep and rocky, and had a lot of bad turns in it, so they decided to put up at the first farmhouse that would take them in.

They could just about see a big boulder that jutted out so that the road had to turn sharp around it, and there on the other side was a little farmhouse with a light in the window. So Mr. Kraft — that was his name: Wilbur Kraft — he pulled the car over to the well-worn tracks of an old driveway. He knocked on the door, and when an elderly couple came to the door he explained how he and his wife were looking for a place to stay, and asked if these folks would put them up for the night.

The old couple looked at each other for a minute and then they told Mr. Kraft that they didn't have much room but they guessed it could be arranged, if the Krafts would take them as they were and not expect anything special. So Mrs. Kraft came in, and

the four of them sat around the little living room talking. The old folks said their name was Butler. They said they'd lived there a long time, and they told the Krafts about the old days on the mountain and how different things were from what they used to be.

Mrs. Kraft kept looking around the room to see if there were any antiques they could buy from the old folks. Over in one corner she sees a kidney-shaped marble-top table. Would the Butlers be willing to sell it? Well, no — it had been a wedding present, and they wouldn't feel they could sell it.

After a little while Mr. Kraft said he thought they would go to bed now, and could he pay for their lodging right then so's they could skin out early in the morning and get on home.

Mr. Butler said, "We talked this over when you went out to get your wife, and we agreed that you would be our guests and that you were to pay us nothing." They argued about it politely for a spell and then they all went to bed.

About five o'clock the Krafts got up and dressed and came downstairs on their tiptoes. He went over to the corner and put a silver dollar on the edge of the marble-top table they had been admiring the night before and went out the door.

They got the car started, and drove down the mountain a couple of miles where they found a little town with a quick-lunch place open. They had some breakfast, and while they were eating, the girl who waited on them got talking to them.

"Come far this morning?" she asks them after a while.

"No, we stayed a couple of miles up the mountain," says Mr. Kraft.

"That so?" she says, "Where'd you stay? I live up there and know just about everybody."

"With a nice old couple named Butler," says Kraft's wife.

"Butler? I never heard of anybody by that name on the mountain. Whereabouts do they live?" she wants to know.

Well, they try to tell her, and she remembers the place in the road but she's bound and determined there isn't a house within a mile of that place. Just then the boss comes into the argument, and when he hears what it's all about, a funny look comes over his face.

"Mister," he says to Kraft, "you're not tryin' to kid us, are you?"

"I don't know what you mean," says Kraft. "I'm telling the simple truth. We spent the night on the mountain with a couple named Butler, at the place in the road where the big boulder sticks way out into the road. And the girl here says we didn't. It's a little silly if you ask me."

The boss was still wearing that funny look. "That's what anybody would think," he said, "only there's more to it. The girl is right. There's not a house within a mile of the big boulder. But, Mister — and this is the funny part — thirty years ago there *was* a house right there, and the couple who lived there *was* named Butler. They both died when the place burned down. I remember the night it burned like it was yesterday."

That settled matters; all four of them got in the boss's car and went back up the mountain, just to see for themselves. What do you 'spose they found? No house. That was clear enough, though they found the tracks in the grass where Kraft had parked his car. But they found the old foundation of the house, all overgrown with weeds and hollyhocks. There were charred timbers and places where the foundation had fallen in. The Krafts just stood there, bug-eyed, looking at the hole in the ground and then at each other. They started to go back to the car when Mrs. Kraft let out a little yip and fainted dead away.

They got some water and brought her around after a bit. All she could say for a few minutes was, "The marble-top. The marble-top!" Then her husband saw it too. Back in the corner of the foundation, in exactly the same position it had occupied in the room, was the kidney-shaped marble-top. The table had long since rotted away.

But there on the edge of the marble, was the silver dollar Kraft had left just a few hours before!

Well, the Krafts high-tailed it for the city, and soon afterward they sold their business. Mrs. Kraft couldn't abide old furniture from that day on.

Nobody ever goes near the old Butler place. There's no house there, of course — nothing but a crumbling foundation, and a beat-up marble table-top. But just the same, people around these parts still call that spot where the Krafts spent the night "the most haunted house."

The Witch
in the Wintry Wood

by Aileen Fisher

This is the story of timid Tim
who thought that witches went after him
when the night was dark and the moon was dim.
Woo-HOO, woo-HOO, woo-HOO.

This is the tale of how Tim one night
didn't start home until candlelight
when the sky was black and the snow was white.
Woo-HOO, woo-HOO, woo-HOO.

He walked through the woods like a frightened goat,
his muffler twisted around his throat,
expecting to jump at a witch's note:
"Woo-HOO, woo-HOO, woo-HOO."

Out of the night came a sheep dog's yowl,
which Tim was sure was a witch's howl,
a terrible witch on a wintry prowl.
Woo-HOO, woo-HOO, woo-HOO.

43

Tim, the timid, began to race,
certain he sighted a witch's face
back of each shadowy hiding place.
Woo-HOO, woo-HOO, woo-HOO.

He ran through the woods on his lonely trek
till horrors! a hand went around his neck,
holding his headlong flight in check.
Woo-HOO, woo-HOO, woo-HOO.

Around his throat went a witch's hand
that jerked poor Tim to a sudden stand.
His heart was water, his legs were sand!
Woo-HOO, woo-HOO, woo-HOO.

Nobody knows how long he stood
with that hand on his throat in the silent wood
until he could find some hardihood . . .
Woo-HOO, woo-HOO, woo-HOO.

Then he looked around like a shaky calf,
thinking of words for his epitaph,
and "Oh, ho, ho!" he began to laugh . . .
Woo-HOO, woo-HOO, woo-HOO.

For what he saw was a funny sight —
it *wasn't* a witch at his throat by night,
but a pine branch pulling his muffler tight!
Woo-HOO, woo-HOO, woo-HOO.

The Ghost Dog of South Mountain

by Frances Carpenter

*P*EOPLE who lived on the South Mountain of the Blue Ridge often saw the black Ghost Dog. At least they said they had seen it.

They told how the Ghost Dog always appeared on the road that led to the Rich Woman's house. How it stood in the way and would not let a man pass. How no horse would go on until the black dog shape melted away into the evening dark.

Many people in South Mountain tried to explain about the black Ghost Dog. Granny always said she knew the true story. Granny should have known. She lived on South Mountain for one hundred years. And she had seen the Rich Woman with her own eyes. This is the way she said it was:

The Rich Woman had a fine stone house on the

side of the mountain. There were green fields around her stone house. She had a big garden, a grape arbor, and an orchard filled with apple and peach trees.

Good fortune seemed to follow that Rich Woman. Her sheep all had twin lambs. Her cows never lost their calves. She sold her apples and peaches for a great deal of money.

What she did with the money, nobody knew. No one ever heard of her spending an extra penny on herself or her two sons.

Where was the husband of the Rich Woman? Granny did not say much about him. But she told of the woman's two sons, who grew up in that fine stone house.

One of these was the good-tempered lad, Adam, whom everyone loved. And the other was Ethan, whom everyone hated.

Adam always had a pleasant "Good morning" for whomever he met on the mountain road. It was good to come upon that smiling young man and his gentle black dog.

In those days the black dog on South Mountain was a friendly, playful puppy, capering about at the heels of his master, the pleasant youth, Adam.

With Ethan it was different. Ethan walked, or rode, all by himself. And always he took more than his half of the road. Without a smile or an "Excuse me," he crowded all he met off to one side.

Ethan had no smiles for his good brother, either.

They said on South Mountain that Ethan hated Adam. They said Ethan's black hate was what drove Adam away from his mother's house.

The Rich Woman cried when Adam went off to seek his fortune on the other side of the Blue Ridge. The neighbors were sorry, too. But saddest of all was Adam's black dog, who had to be left behind.

The dog moped and whined. He lay on the doorstep of the stone house. Always he was looking far down the road to see if his dear master was coming back.

Adam's dog took good care to keep out of the way of the bad-tempered Ethan. The dog knew the hurt of a kick from Ethan's boot, and of a blow from his staff.

The Rich Woman was kind to the black dog, and the dog took to following her about the place. All the day long he walked by her side. All night he slept at the foot of her bed. Into the garden, out in the barn, over the fields, and into the forest that black dog went about with the Rich Woman.

At last one day the Rich Woman felt that her end was not far off. Before she died she wrote down her last wishes on paper. With her pen and strong black ink she wrote, so her words could not be changed:

"My lands shall belong to my two sons. The stone house shall be theirs. But my money shall belong to the one of my sons who finds it." This was the will the Rich Woman left.

Hard-hearted Ethan was secretly glad when his mother was dead.

"Her lands and her house shall be all mine," he said to himself, "for I shall not tell my brother that our mother is dead. It will be a long time before Adam learns of her will. I shall have the first chance to look for her money."

Ethan searched the stone house. He looked all through the cellar. He poked around in the attic. He took up the floor boards. He pulled down the walls of the closets. Indeed, that young man almost tore the stone house to pieces. But he found no treasure.

Ethan was so busy looking for the money that he let the farm work go. There were weeds in the garden. Bugs ruined the fruit. There were no apples or peaches for him to sell.

No money came in now to buy new seeds for the next year. There was not enough food for the farm animals. One by one he sold them, the sheep and the cows, the horses and the pigs.

"I would sell you too, dog," Ethan said to his brother's pet. "But no one would buy you."

The poor dog was thin. He had grown weak because Ethan gave him so little to eat. The black dog lived on rabbits and other small creatures he could catch in the woods. Soon he was almost too weak to run after them.

"Get out of my way," Ethan cried one day in going out the door. "I am sick of your whining." That

49

wicked young man gave the black dog such a blow with his stick that the poor creature died.

"Now at last Adam's dog will be gone from my sight," Ethan said, as he buried the dog's body out in the garden.

But he was wrong. That very night the black dog came into the room where Ethan was going to sleep. From his bed, the man could see the dog standing there, big and black, in the doorway.

Each night, just after sunset, the Ghost Dog would appear. His eyes burned like two red-hot coals of fire. His long tongue was red between his white teeth. Wherever Ethan went after dark, the Ghost Dog was close behind him.

The young man could not rest. All day long he thought of the coming night and how the black Ghost Dog would look at him. At last there was nothing for him to do but go away from the stone house.

"I have looked for my mother's treasure all through this house," Ethan said to the neighbors. "I have looked in the barns. I have even looked under the trough in the pigsty.

"It may be my mother had no money at all, though what she did with all she had I cannot guess. But I am going away from here. As long as the Ghost Dog roams through the stone house, I cannot live here. My brother Adam is welcome to this gloomy

place. May he be just as unhappy here as I have been!"

The very next day Ethan packed up everything he could take with him. He went far, far away, and no one ever saw that bad-tempered young man on South Mountain again.

It was just after Ethan left that the cabin folk began to meet the black Ghost Dog on the roads near the stone house.

"The Ghost Dog is looking for someone," they said. "He surely is watching for his master to come home again."

They were right. It was Adam for whom the Ghost Dog was waiting.

Somehow word of his mother's death went out over the mountains. In spite of Ethan, Adam heard the news. He learned that his brother had nearly torn the stone house to pieces in looking for their mother's treasure. And Adam thought he would just go back and see it all for himself.

On a table in the stone house, Adam found the paper which his mother had written upon. This was her will that said, "My money shall belong to the one of my sons who finds it."

Ethan had left Adam a paper too. His paper said, "If you ever come back, this place is all yours. I want no part of it."

The very first evening Adam was sitting by the table looking at the two papers. Something, or someone, made him look toward the door. There he saw his black dog, wagging his tail.

"Black Boy! Come here!" the young man called out. The Ghost Dog was so real that Adam thought at first it must be alive. But when he laid his hand on the dog's head, he could feel nothing. And his neighbors had already told him how his black dog had died.

Adam saw the Ghost Dog run to the door, then look back at him. When the young man did not rise to follow, the dog ran back again to his side. Again he ran to the door. Again he looked back as if to beg his master to come with him.

So Adam got up and went after his dog out into the moonlight. The dog led him past the barn, through the apple orchard, and into the woods. There, before a small pile of rocks, the Ghost Dog came to a stop. The eerie animal poked his black nose into a hole at the bottom of the pile.

Adam reached into the hole with his stick. There was a ringing sound, as if the stick had touched metal. Then, one after the other, the young man laid the stones aside.

Before his eyes lay a great metal box. What was in it you have already guessed, I am sure. Yes, that great box was full of bright golden coins. It was the treasure that his mother had hidden, and it was a rich treasure.

Granny always said that the Rich Woman wanted

her son Adam to have her money. Why else would she have shown the black dog where she hid it?

Adam sold his mother's farm on the mountainside. Granny said that the reason Adam would not live in the stone house was his brother, Ethan. He was afraid Ethan would return and want to live there with him. Whatever his reason was, Adam went back to the lands beyond the Blue Ridge. And his neighbors on South Mountain never saw him again.

Did the Ghost Dog go away with his master? Or now that he had led his master to the treasure in the woods, did he rest easy in his grave?

Anyway, no one today ever meets the black Ghost Dog on the paths of South Mountain there in the Blue Ridge.

The Thing
at the Foot of the Bed

by Maria Leach

O NCE there was a man, and they dared him to sleep all night in a haunted house.

"All right," he said. He wasn't scared of anything. He'd sleep there. No such thing as ghosts, anyway.

So he went into the house and looked around. Everything looked all right. So he went upstairs. Everything looked all right there too. So he went to bed.

He lay in bed a while and listened. He didn't hear anything. So he went to sleep. It was a warm night, so he had no covers but a sheet.

The man slept a while, and then suddenly he woke up. He listened. He didn't hear anything.

The moon was shining bright through the open window. So — very carefully — very quietly — he looked around. And he saw, down at the foot of the bed, two shiny eyes staring right at him. They looked something like this:

They didn't even blink.

Was that a head — a face?

The man thought he could make out the top of a flat crooked head.

He was *scared*.

He didn't dare move.

But softly, very softly, he slid his hand up under the pillow and pulled out the revolver he'd brought with him.

He aimed at the thing, right between the eyes. He was so scared, though, that his hand trembled and wiggled and shook, and . . .

"E-E-E-E-E-E-K!"

The poor scared fool had shot off his own big toe.

(His feet were sticking out below the sheet, and the moonlight shining on the nails of his big toes looked like two ghostly eyes.)

Ghost in the Orchard

by *Aileen Fisher*

*F*REDDY tiptoed across the creaky kitchen floor and looked out the window. The stars were bright. Above the hills hung a piece of moon like a round white cracker with a big bite taken out. The potato patch seemed almost light behind the row of currant bushes now bare of leaves.

Freddy could see as far as the orchard. But there the shadows began — right where the ghost liked to move about among the apple trees!

Many of the apple trees still had their leaves, browned by late-October frosts, clinging stubbornly to the branches. And some of the trees still had late apples. But the ghost did not seem to like to climb up into the high branches where the best apples hung. It stayed on the ground, white and graceful, drifting in and out among the trees. At least that is what it did the two times Freddy had seen it — once last week and again two nights ago.

Freddy hadn't breathed a word about his ghost to anyone. Pop would be sure to say it was only a dream. Mom would say it was that extra piece of cake — she *knew* Freddy shouldn't eat another piece of cake! And his two little sisters — well, they were too young to know about ghosts anyway. Besides, Freddy had to get one really good look before he was sure himself.

The wind blew a thin white scarf of cloud over the moon. That made the potato patch darker and the orchard even more shadowy than before. Then the bony fingers of a poplar branch began to scratch against the window sill. Scratch, scratch!

Freddy stood still as stone at the window and watched. He was not sure if he wanted the ghost to come. With Mom and Pop at the Grange meeting, and the two little girls sound asleep upstairs, he was all alone. But as long as the ghost stayed out in the orchard and he was safe in the house, it would be all right.

Tick, tick, tick! went the clock on top of the stove, as loud as if it were ticking through a loud-speaker. Freddy creaked across the floor to see what time it was. Almost nine. Mom told him they wanted to find him in bed when they got home around nine thirty. Well, the ghost had better hurry.

Freddy went to the window again. Pop had left the barn door open, so the building looked like a big face with its mouth open — a mouth full of darkness.

Just then something like the swish of a ghost brushed against Freddy's leg. He jumped! His throat seemed to close up, pinching off his voice.

Then it came again, that brush against his leg. Freddy held his breath and heard his heart thumping in his ears.

For the third time his leg was touched. But now there was a familiar purring sound with it that set Freddy's heart to beating in the right place once more. He gave a big sigh of relief and stooped down.

"Mouser," he said, "you scared me out of a year's growth. I thought you were a ghost! How did you get in here? You're supposed to be out in the barn catching mice." Mouser arched her back and purred and rubbed herself some more.

At the window again, Freddy felt much braver with Mouser around. Not that Mouser had ever caught a ghost. But just to know she was close and awake, that was something. Wait! What was that? What was that white thing out in the orchard, gliding behind the trunks of the trees? It must be the ghost! What else could it be? Freddy pressed his forehead against the cold glass and strained his eyes, trying to get a good look.

The moon was sailing free of clouds again for a

minute. But the ghost had a teasing way of staying in the shadows, back in the orchard, instead of moving out into the open. For a fleeting second Freddy caught the glint of moonlight on its head. Was it really a head, or a hat with some strange decorations? He had never heard of a ghost wearing a hat, still . . .

There was a sudden noise at the front of the house. Freddy drew back from the window and listened. Someone, or something, was at the front door. What was this anyway, with a ghost in the orchard and a knock at the front door?

Freddy tiptoed toward the living room, where the lights were still lit. Quickly he ducked into the bedroom which opened off to one side. From there he could see the front door, see who was knocking. He peeked out.

Knock, knock! Well, it wasn't a ghost at least. Instead of being flimsy and white, it was big and black and wore a wide-brimmed hat. That hat! Freddy knew it at once. It belonged to Big Pete who lived in a log cabin back toward the hills, Big Pete who helped Pop whenever there was extra work on the farm.

Freddy hurried to the front door and opened it. "Hello," he said. "Sorry I didn't get here sooner. I was out in the kitchen."

"Your Pa home, is he? Coming up from town I saw your lights still on and figured I'd find out where your Pa wanted the poles put that I cut over on Red Hill . . ." Big Pete talked in a tone of voice that never went up and never went down, but just stayed straight and flat like a pavement, running on and on.

"Mom and Pop went to the Grange meeting. But they won't be late." Freddy stopped. Part of him wanted Big Pete to stay and talk, and another part wanted him to go. If Big Pete stayed, Freddy wouldn't be all alone with the ghost. On the other hand, he wouldn't be able to get a good look at it with company around. "Ah . . . won't you come in and wait?" he finished.

"Guess I'll be moving along. It's pretty late for me to be up and about of a night, and I can stop by and see your Pa in the morning about the poles." Big Pete turned to go. "Cut a nice lot of spruce poles for him on the north slope of Red Hill. Nothing like a north slope to make good spruce poles."

"Wait a minute." Freddy wasn't sure just what he wanted to say to Big Pete. Still, he didn't want him to go quite yet. "Do you . . . do you believe in ghosts?"

Big Pete turned back and looked at Freddy, who tried to keep from shivering as he stood in the open doorway with the night air upon him. "You ain't seen any around here, have you? Can't say as I either believe in them or don't believe in them — but my grandmother now, she was a great one for believing in ghosts, she was."

"Won't you come in a minute? It's cold, and I'd like to know about your grandmother."

"Reckon I can stay a minute or two if you're a mind to hear about ghosts," Big Pete drawled. He kept right on talking, with his voice in a straight line, as he came in the door and stood there while Freddy quickly closed it. "My grandmother, she was on real friendly terms with ghosts, she was — always talking to them and seeing them sitting around the house."

"Around the house!"

"Yep, and especially the ghost of her mother sitting in her special rocking chair in the front room, just like she used to sit when my grandmother was a girl."

Freddy looked out of the corner of his eye at the nearby chairs. "Did your grandmother's ghost ever wear a hat?"

"Not that I ever heard tell of. My grandmother used to see her mother plain as day sitting there, though no one else in the family ever could. Something about my grandmother made her see things other folks couldn't."

"I'd rather have the ghosts stay outside somewhere . . . like in the orchard. Did your grandmother ever see any in your orchard?"

"Not that I recall she didn't. I never heard of any

63

ghosts sticking around any orchards." Big Pete kept turning his hat around and around in his hands, as if talking about ghosts made him a little nervous. "Well I reckon you better stop thinking about ghosts, boy, or you won't get any sleep tonight and me neither." He put his hand on the doorknob. "You ain't scared to stay here till your folks get home, are you?"

"Me? No. Why, I take care of the place lots of times." Freddy tried to sound brave, but he didn't feel so brave inside.

"You can tell your Pa I'll be down to see him about the poles in the morning — nice straight poles off the north side of Red Hill." Still talking, he went out into the night and closed the door behind him.

Freddy took a deep breath. He gave a sideways glance at the old rocker with its padded seat, and was glad to see that it was empty. Would the ghost still be waiting out in the orchard, he wondered? Or would it be frightened away?

He tiptoed into the dark kitchen again to take up his post at the window. The poplar fingers were still scratching against the sill, and the clock was still ticking loudly. Unfortunately another cloud had slipped over the moon, like a soft wool muffler that held back the light except around the edges.

Freddy closed his eyes for a moment to get used to the darkness. Then he stared toward the orchard. Sure enough, the ghost was still there! He could see

the light-colored figure moving behind the trees. Moving toward the potato patch!

Slowly, gracefully, the ghost glided out into the open. And for the first time Freddy got a good look — as good a look as the dim moonlight would permit. "Whewww," he said to himself. "If it was closer to Christmas, I'd think it was one of . . . But, of course, it couldn't be. How could it?"

Suddenly, for no apparent reason except curiosity, the ghost began to glide toward the open mouth of the barn. It walked lightly, as if the earth were made of air and feathers. Freddy heard his heart jumping around in his ears again. He opened and closed his hands. If the ghost went into the barn . . . maybe . . . maybe, Freddy thought, he could slip out quietly and close the door. Maybe he could catch a ghost!

In front of the open hole of darkness the ghost paused, holding its headdress high. Then it walked into the mouth of shadows.

Freddy gasped. There was no time to be afraid! He knew he would have to move quickly and quietly. If he went out the back way, he might make too much noise. So, trembling with excitement, he hurried to the living room and slipped out the front door.

Underfoot the short-clipped sod was soft and quiet. Carefully he ducked around the house, keeping in the shadows. He would have to make a break for the barn, after leaving the last shadow. What if the ghost tried to rush out before Freddy could close the door?

Freddy darted forward. Quickly he slid the heavy door halfway, then fully shut. He felt hot all over, although the night was chilly and he had come out without a coat. "Whewww," he sighed. He had caught a ghost!

Back in the house, Freddy looked at the clock. Nine fifteen. He would have to hurry if he was to get to bed by nine thirty, the way Mom expected. But he would have to warn Pop not to put the car in the barn. How could he? A sign! That was it. He would print a sign and tack it to the barn door.

He took the cardboard from the back of his school tablet and a piece of black crayon and wrote "WARNING." Then he stopped. How did you spell "ghost"? He knew there was an h in it somewhere, but where? Well, there wasn't time to look it up. He bent over the cardboard:

WARNING!

GOHST INSIDE

DO NOT OPEN THE DOOR

Then he found some tacks in the nail box and went out to put up the sign.

After a night of tossing and turning, Freddy woke up when he heard Mom and Pop stirring about in the kitchen. The first thing he did was to look out the window. Good! The car was parked in front of the barn. The door was still closed and the sign still in place. The ghost . . . but now that it was daylight, Freddy wasn't so sure about the ghost. He wondered if he had dreamed it, after all.

"What's all this nonsense about not opening the barn door?" Pop asked when Freddy came into the kitchen.

"And what is a G-O-H-S-T?" asked Mom, standing by the stove watching the toast. "Did you walk in your sleep? I *told* you not to eat too much cake last night."

The little girls looked from Freddy to Mom to Pop, wondering what it was all about. Their eyes bulged when Freddy began to tell his story — about the ghost in the orchard, how it went into the barn, how he sneaked out and closed the door.

"Humph," Pop said, and came over to put his hand on Freddy's forehead. "You don't seem to have a fever, son. Stick out your tongue. Hmmm. Looks all right. What kind of ghost did you say it was?"

"Well . . . maybe it sounds crazy . . . but it looked like the ghost of something that belongs to Santa Claus."

Pop gave Freddy a queer look. "Come on out, boy. We'll have to look into this. We can go through the workshop, so we won't disturb your *ghost.*"

Ten minutes later Freddy and his father were back in the house, all excited.

"What is it?" Mom asked anxiously.

"Get the long-distance operator and have her put through a call to the Denver Zoo at City Park." Pop never liked to talk on the telephone; he always made Mom do it. "We've got to talk to somebody there."

"About the ghost?"

"About the ghost," Pop answered, as Mom went to the phone. "I've got to find out if they know anything about it. It's the strangest creature I ever saw. Freddy's right. It looks like the ghost of one of Santa Claus's reindeer — the kind you see in pictures. Only this one's real. It's breathing-real and alive."

"It's a little pale-yellow deer with regular reindeer antlers," Freddy said.

"Not a bit like our mule-deer around here," Pop put in.

Freddy laughed. "You can see why it looked like a ghost, light-colored like that, behind the trees in the orchard. Only I thought it had on a fancy hat."

Mom finally got the call through to the zoo and the right person on the other end. And before long the mystery of Freddy's ghost was all cleared up. It was a fallow deer, from England. Several fallow deer had escaped from the zoo some months before and lost themselves in the hills.

"It must have liked your apples," the man from the zoo said. "We'll be over to pick it up this afternoon. That's some boy you have, folks . . . catching a ghost single-handed!"

The Golden Arm

by Maria Leach

This scary story is a favorite for telling around a campfire, or on Halloween. When you tell it, be sure to wait a minute where it says to pause. Someone will certainly scream at the unexpected ending!

O NCE there was a man who had a woman for a wife named Elvira, and this woman had a golden arm. She was awful proud of it. It was solid shining gold from the shoulder clear down to the nail of her little finger. She liked it even better than the real one.

Every night when she went to bed she used to say to her husband, "If I die first, promise to bury me with my golden arm."

"Yes, Elviry, I promise," the man would say, night after night after night.

Well, it happened that the woman got sick and died. The man buried her and her golden arm along with her, just as he had promised.

But after a while he began to think about it. He began to think about what he could do with all that gold. It seemed a shame for it just to lie there in the ground. He began to *want* the golden arm. And the more he thought about it, the more he wanted it.

So one dark night in the middle of the night he decided to go get it. He put on his long, dark coat, and he lighted his lantern and went trudging through the cold, dark lanes till he came to the graveyard. And he dug up Elvira and took the golden arm.

He tucked it under his long coat and started back home. On the way home it started to rain, hail, snow, and blow. But he didn't think anything of that. He got home all right.

When he got home, he didn't know where to hide the golden arm, so he pushed it under the covers of the bed. Then he jumped into bed himself and shivered and shook. He couldn't get warm because the golden arm was cold as ice.

And the wind rose and he heard a voice wailing:

W-H-E-E-R-E'-S M-Y G-O-O-L-D-E-N A-A-A-R-M?

The man pulled the covers up over his head so he wouldn't hear it. But he heard it just the same.

He heard it coming down the road. It was crying in the road:

W-H-E-E-R-E'-S M-Y-Y

. . . and on the porch . . .

G-O-O-L-D-E-N

. . . and at the door . . .

A-A-A-R-M?

And the wind howled over the top of the door:

W-H-E-E-R-E'-S M-Y G-O-L-D-E-N A-A-R-M?

The man shivered and shook under the covers. Then he peeked out.

And he saw it.

It was by the bed.

And — (*pause*) — it pounced!

YOU'VE GOT IT!

The Ghosts
from the Graveyard

by Sorche Nic Leodhas

THERE was once a young doctor of learning who was sore troubled with bogles. He was the only son of an old couple to whom he had been born when they were getting along in years. They were determined to make a man of learning of him and had the brass to pay for it, so he had been little at home since he was a bit of a lad, being off and away at one school or another most of his days. He went to day school, and to grammar school, then to a Scottish public school. Then he went to the University of Edinboro', and after that to various universities here and there about the face of Europe. While he was away getting all this schooling, his mother and father got older and older, and at last they got so old they died of it, both satisfied that they'd done their best for their son.

By that time he'd got all the knowledge he thought he needed, and he decided it was time to come home to the house his parents had left him and write a book about all the things he'd learned.

So back he came and settled into the house.

He found that it was a dreary old house in a dreary old street in the heart of the old part of Dundee, where the smoke from all the chimneys of the town had hung over it for long, long years. The Dundee Law building seemed to tower over it and want to shut it in, although it was really not so near as it looked. But the house stood close by the Howff, that ancient graveyard which has held the honored and famous dead of the town for over three hundred years.

The house was as dark and dismal inside as it was without. The walls were dark and damp, and of no sort of color you could lay a name to. There were great wooden blinds to the windows that kept the light out, for his mother had always said the light would fade the carpet.

Why he should stay there in the dank old place at an age when other young men were out enjoying themselves was a queer sort of riddle. Maybe he couldn't have told the answer to it himself, if he'd ever thought about it at all.

There was no lack of money, for he'd been left plenty. But he was a quiet, steady young man and his wants were few, and maybe he was just glad to settle down in peace after all the traveling around from one school to another. So he took the house the way it was and let it be.

When he settled in, he looked about till he found himself a cook and a lass to keep house for him. The two of them came with their boxes and took over. But after they'd been there a day or two the cook came to him and said, "There's somewhat amiss with the garret, maister."

"What would it be?" he asked.

"The draughts is terrible," she told him. "Ye canna keep a door ajar but a breeze comes by and bangs it shut. And the locks won't hold, for as soon as it's shut the draught bangs it wide open again. What with banging and creaking all the night, the lass and me can get no sleep at all!"

"Well, move down to the next story," said the doctor. "I'll have in a man to look to the garret."

The man came and looked to the garret, but he could find naught wrong, for the windows were tight and he couldn't find the sign of a place for the draught to come in.

But a few days later the doctor came down to his breakfast to find the boxes of the two women in the hall and the women beside them, white as winding sheets.

The cook spoke for both of them. "We'll be leaving ye, maister," said she, "this very morning's morn!"

"Why then?" asked the astonished doctor.

"We'll not be staying in a place where there's bogles!" said the cook firmly. The serving lass shrieked a wee shriek and rolled her eyes and clutched the cook's arm.

"Bogles!" The doctor laughed. "You mean ghosts? Oh come, come now! You are a sensible woman. You know there are no such things as ghosts!"

"I know what I know!" said the cook.

Then the two of them picked up their boxes and out of the door they went, without waiting to ask could they get their wages!

Well, that was the way it was after that. The doctor would find himself a new couple of women to look after the house. They'd come with their boxes and all, but after a few days the boxes were down in the hall and the women beside them, ready to go their ways, and all because of the bogles!

Two by two they came, and two by two they went, over and over again, and not even the promise of better wages would tempt them to stay.

And at last came a time when the doctor could find no one who would come at all, for the ones who left had spread the news wide and there wasn't a lass in the town of Dundee who'd step a foot into the doctor's house. No! Not even for all the money in Dundee!

Then the doctor took the ferry over the Tay to Newport, thinking maybe he could find a cook and housemaid there. But the news of the doctor's bogles had got to Newport before him, being the sort of news that travels fast. The Newport lassies who were willing to go into service would have nothing at all to do with him, after they found out who he was.

It came into his mind then that he'd heard they had a wheen of ghosts in St. Andrews. Maybe the women there'd be used to them, and wouldn't mind a house that was said to have bogles in it.

Not that he believed in bogles himself. No indeed. Not he!

So he made the journey from Newport to St. Andrews. But he had no luck there at all. There were bogles galore, 'tis true. In fact the place must have been teeming with them, for, the folks at St. Andrews told him proudly, there was scarcely a house in the town that hadn't a bogle or two in it — certainly not one of the older houses.

But the trouble with St. Andrews was that if there were no lack of bogles, there were no lassies who weren't already in service. And they all said they were suited fine where they were, thank you, and wouldn't like to be making a change, even for the bigger wages the doctor was willing to pay.

So it looked as if he'd just have to do for himself, though he didn't know how to cook at all; and as for cleaning up and making things tidy, he knew less about that.

He started back home again, for there was nothing else he could do.

When he was on the ferry going back from Newport to Dundee he saw a lass on the boat. She was the sort of a lass you look twice at, for she had the reddest hair in the world, springing up in wee curls in the fresh wind from the Tay. She had the white skin that goes with that sort of hair, and a saucy nose with a sprinkle of freckles across it, and eyes of the bluest blue he'd ever seen.

She was neat as a silver pin, too, with a little flat straw hat pinned tight to her curls and a white blouse and a tidy black skirt. But what he noticed most was her smile, for it was merry and kind.

He thought she wouldn't be minding if he went and spoke to her. So he went over and stood beside her at the rail of the boat.

"Do you believe in bogles?" he asked her.

She looked at him and her eyes crinkled, and she broke into a laugh. "Och, do I not!" she cried. "My old grannie at Blairgowrie that I'm going to stay with had a rare time with a pair of them a year or so back, till she rid them out!"

"Oh," said he.

"Do you not believe in them?" asked the red-haired lass curiously.

"No I don't!" said he.

And that was the end of that, for if she believed

79

in bogles there was no use asking her to come and keep house for him, because she would not stay any more than the rest of them.

When he got back home, he went into the scullery to see what there was for his supper. But what was there that had to be cooked he didn't know what to do with. He just had to make do with the heel of a loaf of bread and a bit of stale cheese that wasn't fit to bait a mousetrap with.

So when he went into his study he was hungry and he was tired and he was plain put about!

He sat down at his desk and banged his fist on it, and he shouted out loud! " 'Tis all nonsense! THERE ARE NO BOGLES!"

"Oh, aren't there?" asked a quiet voice behind him.

He whirled around in his chair, and then his eyes bugged out and his hair stood straight up on his head.

There were three big white things standing there, *and he could see right through them.*

But the doctor was awful stubborn. "There are no bogles," he said again, only his voice wasn't so loud this time, and he didn't sound as if he was so sure about it.

"Then what would you be calling us?" asked one of them politely.

Well, there was no two ways about it. Bogles they were, and BOGLES he had to call them. So he had to admit that there *were* bogles in his house.

What he didn't know yet was how many of them were there. Because they liked his house fine. It was so nice and dark and damp.

It was not so bad as far as his meals went, for he was taking them at the inn, rather than starve at home. But at home he was fair distracted, for it seemed as if there were more and more bogles all the time.

Bogles peered down at him from over the rail of the staircase, and there were always some of them lurking about in the corners of any room he was in, blinking their eyes at him and sighing at him, and they gave him a chill. The three first ones followed him about, and when he went up to his bed at night they came along and sat on the foot of the bed and talked to him.

They all came from the Howff, they told him.

"Och aye," sighed one of them. " 'Twas a fine graveyard, one time."

"For the first hundred years or so," said the second bogle.

"But after that it began to get crowded. A lot of new people got brought in, and some of them wasn't the sort we'd want to neighbor with," said the first one again.

But since they had found his place, they told the doctor, 'twas far better. They liked it fine in his house and all the best bogles were moving over there too, so they felt much more at home than they did in the Howff.

Things being the way they were, the doctor had no peace by day or by night. He was writing away on his learned book about some sort of wisdom or other, I wouldn't know what. He was having a hard time of it, for the bogles were that curious that they hung about him and peered over his shoulder, and even took to criticizing what he wrote. One of them even got so familiar that he'd lean on the doctor's shoulder and point out places where the doctor could be doing better with his words. It annoyed the doctor a lot, because he found himself writing down what the bogle said, and he had ideas of his own that he liked better than the ones the bogle was giving him.

One day as he sat in the inn eating his dinner, he made up his mind that he'd take no more of the bogles, for he had had enough!

So he went home and put on his best clothes for a journey, and off he went to Blairgowrie to find the red-haired lass and ask her what her grannie had done to rid herself of her bogles.

When he got to Blairgowrie, he went about the town looking for the lass. He couldn't ask for her, for he didn't know her name. By and by he got to the end of the town, and there he saw a neat little two-story cottage with a low stone wall around it, and inside of the wall a big garden full of flowers. There was a bench by the door of the cottage, and

on the bench sat the red-haired lass, and she was still smiling.

"Good day!" says he.

"Good day!" says she. "I thought you'd soon be coming along."

"You did!" said he, surprised. "Why did you then?"

"Because you asked if I believed in bogles. So then I knew that you had some of your own and would be coming to find out what my grannie did to get rid of hers."

He was amazed that one so bonny could be so wise. So he opened the gate and went into the garden. He sat down on the bench beside her and told her all his troubles.

"Will you come and help me get them out of the house?" he asked, when he'd finished his story.

"Of course I will!" said she.

Then she took him in to her grannie. Her grannie was just like her, only her hair was white and she wasn't so young, but her eyes were just as blue and her smile was as merry and kind.

"Grannie," said the lass, "I'm going with this gentleman to keep house for him, and to rid him of some bogles he has at home."

"If anyone can, you can!" said her grannie, and the two of them laughed as if bogles were no trouble at all.

So the lass got ready and off she went with the doctor.

When he opened the door of his house and they went in, the lass wrinkled her nose and made a face. "Faugh!" said she. "It smells of bogle! A proper graveyard smell," she added, looking around at the place.

"They come from the Howff," he told her, as if that explained it.

"I'll be bound!" she said. "And to the Howff they'll go back!"

That night the doctor ate his meal at home, instead of going to the inn. It was a good one, too, for the lass got it, and nobody had ever said that she didn't know how to cook.

There wasn't a sign of a bogle that night, but that was because they were biding their time and looking the lass over.

The next morning the lass came into the study. She had on a blue overall, the same color as her eyes, and there was a fresh white kerchief tied to cover her hair.

"This is a proper dark old place," said she, looking about the room. "Why do you not throw back those big old blinds and open the windows to let a wee bit of sun and fresh air in?"

"My mother said it would let dust in and fade the carpets," the doctor said. He remembered that from the time when he was a wee lad, before he went off to his schools.

85

"What if it does!" said she. "Can you not buy new ones?"

"I never thought of that!" he said. "Of course I can."

So the lass pulled the curtains back and folded back the wooden blinds. Then she opened the windows wide and the sea air came pouring in from the harbor, with the sun riding on top of it.

"That's better!" the lass told him.

"It is, indeed!" said the doctor, as he took a long, deep breath of the fresh cool air.

But the red-haired lass took another look at the dingy old room and frowned. "No wonder you have bogles," she said. "I never saw a place they'd like better. But I can do no more for you till time for your dinner, so I'll leave you. I'm turning out the scullery."

So the doctor worked at his book and the lass worked at the scullery, and the day went by.

That night the bogles came in a crowd and gathered around the doctor's bed.

"Who is the red-haired lass in the house?" asked the first bogle.

"She's my new housekeeper," the doctor told them, yawning because he had worked awful hard on his learned book all day. The bogles hadn't come near him because they didn't like all the sunlight that came into the study after the lass opened the windows.

"Is she going to stay here?" they asked.

"I hope so!" yawned the doctor. He had had a good supper, and he'd eaten a lot of it, and now he was so sleepy he couldn't keep his eyes open. Before the bogles had time to ask him anything else he'd fallen fast asleep.

They couldn't wake him for all they tried. So they gave him up and went to see could they scare the red-haired lass away, the same as they had the others. But she had worked hard and eaten well too, so they couldn't waken her, no more than they could the doctor. They all agreed it was a bad day for the bogles when the lass came into the house. It was going to take an awful lot of hard work to get her out again.

The next day the red-haired lass was up early, and the day after that, and the next day after too. The kitchen and the scullery were beginning to look like different places, for she swept and dusted and scrubbed and scoured and polished from morn to night. The doctor saw little of her except at meal-times, but the meals were the best he'd ever had in his life, and she sat across the table from him and poured his tea and smiled at him.

At night he and the lass were so tired out, him with his writing and her with her turning out, that they couldn't be bothered about the bogles.

The bogles were there, nonetheless. They'd brought a lot more bogles from the Howff to help them —

even some of the riffraff they'd moved to the doctor's house to get away from! There were plenty of dark old rooms in the house still, for the lass was still busy with the scullery and the kitchen, and hadn't come off the ground floor yet.

So at night the bogles tried all their best tricks that never had failed before. They swept through the house like a tempest, banging doors open and shut, wailing and gibbering, moaning and mowing, clanking chains and rattling bones, and the like.

It all did no good. Nobody heard them except maybe a passer-by in the street, who thought it was the wind rising from the sea and hurried home so as not to get caught in a storm.

When the end of the week came along, the red-haired lass said to the doctor, "You'd best take your pens and paper and things over to my grannie's at Blairgowrie and do your writing there. I'm through with the kitchen and the scullery, and now I'm going to turn out the rest of the house."

He didn't want to go, but she told him he'd got to for he'd only be in her way.

"You can leave me some money to get some things I'll be needing, and to pay for help to come in, to do what I can't do myself," she told him. "And don't come back till I send for you, mind!"

So he packed up, and off he went to her grannie's house as she told him to.

As soon as he was gone, the red-haired lass started

in again, and now she really showed what she could do. The bogles were so upset about what was going on that one night they laid for her and caught her on the stairs as she was going up to her bed. They tried to look as grisly as they could, and the noises they made were something horrible.

But the red-haired lass only stared straight through them. "Go away, you nasty things!" she said.

"We won't then!" they said indignantly. "We got here first, and we've a mind to stay. Why don't you go away?"

"I like my work and I'm useful here," said the lass. "Which is more than you can say."

"It was all fine till you came," complained one of the bogles.

"It was all wrong till I came," said the lass right back at them. "And I wish you'd stop argy-bargying and let me get to my bed. I've a big day's work ahead of me tomorrow, for the painters are coming in and the men to take away the blinds, and when they're done 'twill be all sunny and bright and a treat to see!"

All the bogles groaned like one big groan.

"Sunny!" moaned one.

"Bright!" shrieked another.

"Well anyway, we're not going away," said they.

"Stay if you like," said the lass. "It's all one to me if you stay or go. But you won't like it!" she promised them. And with that she walked straight up the steps and through the lot of them, and went to bed and to sleep.

After that the battle between the bogles and the lass really began. You couldn't say they didn't put up a fight for it, but the lass was more than a match for them. She drove them from the first story of the house to the second, and from the second to the third, and from the third to the garret, for they couldn't stand the sunlight and brightness that followed her as she went up through the house at her work.

At last they had to pack up their extra winding sheets, and their chains and bones and things, and go back to the graveyard they'd come from, for the house wasn't fit for a bogle to stay in, and even if the Howff was crowded, it suited them better now.

Well, when the painters and carpenters and all were gone the lass found a serving maid to help her with the work. And this one stayed! But the lass didn't bother to look for a cook, for she thought her own cooking would suit the doctor best when he came back to his house.

The doctor was just as comfortable in her grannie's house and just as well fed there, and everything was fine except that he missed the red-haired lass, for he'd begun to get used to having her around. There were no bogles to bother him at the lass's grannie's house, for she had rid herself of hers a long time ago. It came to his mind that he hadn't seen much of his own bogles lately, but he didn't miss them at all.

A week went by and then a second one and a third one. And the doctor found that instead of writing his learned book he'd be sitting and thinking how bright the red-haired lass's hair looked with the sun on it, or how blue her eyes were, or how the freckles looked on her saucy little nose. He was that homesick for her he'd even have put up with the bogles, just to be at home, with her pouring out his tea and smiling at him from across the table.

So when she sent word at the end of the fourth week that he was to come back, he went off so fast that he almost forgot to thank her grannie for having him and to say good-bye!

When he got back to his house, he had to step out into the road and look well at it, for he wasn't sure it was his.

The windows were open from ground floor to garret, and all the heavy wooden blinds had been taken away entirely. There were fresh white curtains blowing gently at all the windows, and flowerpots on the sills.

Then the door opened and the red-haired lass stood in the doorway and smiled at him. It was his house after all!

"You've come then!" said she.

"I've come!" said he. And up the steps he went,

two at a time. He could hardly believe 'twas the same place, when he saw what she'd done with it. Everything was light and bright, and through the whole house the fresh sea air blew, in one window and out another, so that the place was as sweet and fresh and wholesome as the red-haired lass herself.

"How about the bogles?" asked the doctor.

"They're gone," said the lass.

"All of them? Where did they go?" asked the doctor.

"Back to the Howff, I suppose," said the lass. "This isn't the sort of place bogles would be liking to bide in."

"No!" said the doctor, looking around. "I can see that for myself."

But he had one more question to ask, so he asked it. "Will you marry me?" he said.

"Of course I will!" said the red-haired lass. And she smiled at him and said, "Why else did you think I came here in the first place?"

So they were married, and the doctor had no more bogles in his house. But what he did have was half a dozen bairns, lads and lassies, all with red hair and blue eyes and saucy noses with freckles across them and merry smiles, just like their mother.

And bairns are better to fill a house with than bogles ever could be, so they all lived merrily ever after.